Xavier Garza

PIÑATA BOOKS
ARTE PÚBLICO PRESS
HOUSTON, TEXAS

This volume is made possible through grants from the City of Houston through the Houston Arts Alliance.

Piñata Books are full of surprises!

Arte Público Press
University of Houston
452 Cullen Performance Hall
Houston, Texas 77204-2004

Cover and text art by Xavier Garza
Cover design by Giovanni Mora

♾ The paper used in this publication meets the requirements of the American National Standard for Information Sciences—Permanence of Paper for Printed Library Materials, ANSI Z39.48-1984.

Printed in the United States of America
February 2019–March 2019
Versa Press, Inc., East Peoria, IL
10 9 8 7 6

To my parents Margarito and Amalia Garza.
To my sisters Veronica and Vanessa.
To my wife Irma.
To everyone who believed in me.

Table of Contents

Acknowledgments

There are so many people for me to thank that it is hard to know where to begin, but to get the proverbial ball rolling I will start with Tony Díaz, author of *The Aztec Love God*, and founder of Nuestra Palabra in Houston, Texas. It was Tony who first invited me to the Latino Book and Family Festival in Houston where I met Dr. Nicolás Kanellos of Arte Público Press. A brief conversation with him set the foundation for the book you now hold in your hands. For that reason, I thank Dr. Kanellos and the wonderful staff at Arte Público Press for giving me the opportunity to realize my lifelong dream of being a published author. I also want to send out a great big *abrazo* to my literary *compadres* and *comadre* David Rice, Rene Saldana, David Champion, and Marisa Taylor for believing and supporting me. Your words of encouragement over the years have meant a lot to me. I also have a deep appreciation for the Rio Grande Valley where I grew up. I draw my stories of things that go bump in the night from this landscape. A heartfelt *muchas gracias* to my parents and grandparents for filling my head with so many *cucuy* stories that will surely help me to never run out of material to work with. A big I love you and thank you to my wife Irma who has always supported me in what I do. Also thanks to God and to each and every person who has believed in me over the years.

What Is a *Cucuy?*

Have you ever been too scared to sleep with the lights off, or have you mistaken the blowing wind for a woman crying? Did your parents ever tell you that if you were not a good boy or girl, El Cucuy was going to come and get you? El Cucuy, for those who may not know, is one of the many words used to describe the supernatural beings that adults call on to scare their children into being good. La Llorona, *los duendes*, *El Chupacabras,* and the Devil are a few of the dozens of scary beings who appear in these popular tales. These stories tend to have a moral to them, often warning children of the misfortune that will come their way should they disobey their parents or be disrespectful to them in any way. *Cucuys,* however, are not only to be found in Latino culture. Oh no, you can rest assured that every culture has their own *cucuy* stories. Some may call them myths, legends, or downright superstitious nonsense, but in every culture there are individuals who claim these stories to be true.

Xavier Garza

Duendes

Orphaned since birth, Elías San Miguel and Julián Maldonado had spent most of their lives living at the Saint Carol's Home for Boys. Having met three years earlier, the two eleven-year-olds had become as close as brothers, so close that one was seldom seen without the other. The two boys were always ready to lend a helping hand to grownups or share their toys with other children. Yet one day, Elías began to notice that Julián's attitude about being nice to other people had begun to change. Julián was becoming less friendly and had even begun to get into fights with the other boys. As disturbing as his friend's sudden change of behavior was, it was not as bizarre as the fact that several times, Elías had walked in on his troubled friend as he was talking to himself.

One day, Elías decided to confront Julián and ask him what was going on with him.

"Who are you talking to, anyway?" Elías asked Julián, whom he had found staring blankly at the wall in the room that they both shared.

"I am talking to my new friend," Julián replied coldly.

"New friend?" asked Elías, puzzled by his friend's

answer. The wall was Julián's new friend? Elías wondered.

"But it's just a wall," said Elías.

"No," corrected Julián, "it's my special friend's home."

Julián's words troubled Elías, for they reminded him of the stories that Sister Marie, an old nun who had once worked at the home for boys, had told him. She had warned him that children, especially those with no parents, had to be very vigilant to avoid coming under the bad influence of a *duende*.

"A *duende*?" Elías had asked her, never having heard the word before.

Sister Marie explained that a *duende* was an evil troll that most parents wrongly mistook for their child's imaginary friend.

"If you see a boy or girl talking to themselves," Sister Marie had warned, "it could be that a *duende* is on the prowl and is trying to lure the child into doing evil deeds." Sister Marie explained that *duendes* had existed for years and had always operated in secrecy from adults, who seldom saw these small, green-skinned and red-eyed beings. She warned that they would always seek out the most neglected of all children, tricking them into committing unspeakable acts that would get them in trouble. Elías had seen no green-skinned or red-eyed little beings lurking about, so he dismissed Sister Marie's stories.

Julián, however, still showed all the signs of being a child under the influence of a *duende*. His behavior was erratic and rebellious, and he was constantly lying or using foul language, something he had never done before. Julián's change of behavior had begun shortly after a family from Laredo adopted little Jessie Herrera only two months after being placed at the orphanage. Julián had felt that it was unfair for Jessie to find a family so soon after arriving, especially when Julián had been at the orphanage for years without being chosen for adoption.

As he watched Julián stare blankly at a wall, Elías had to wonder if perhaps his friend had lost all his marbles.

"It's just a wall," said Elías. "I don't see anybody."

"Look closer," said Julián, gesturing for Elías to move closer to the wall.

Elías took two steps closer to the empty wall, but still saw nothing.

"Closer," said Julián, his voice filled with a soft, but cackling laughter.

Elías placed his nose mere inches from the wall. "I still see nothing," he began saying, but stopped after noticing a small hole the size of a pinprick in the wall.

"Look into the hole," instructed Julián, "look into the hole."

It was then that a pair of green hands reached out through the wall and grabbed Elías by the head! Elías tried to scream, but lost his voice when he saw a green face with glowing red eyes staring back at him!

"Julián!" Elías began to cry out, asking his friend for help.

Julián just stared at Elías, a cold and malevolent look

frozen in his eyes. It was then, in the blink of an eye, that Elías was sucked into the hole in the wall that was the size of a pinprick!

It seems Julián had been under the influence of a *duende,* and he wanted to become a *duende* himself, to be literally transformed into a green-skinned and red-eyed monster who would prey on other children. So young Julián had sacrificed Elías to the creature to prove that he had the cruelty and evilness to become a *duende* himself. After all, you have to be pretty evil to sacrifice your best friend to a *duende.* Julián disappeared from the orphanage that same day, and he was never seen again.

Another *Duende* Story

Juanito Morín had been an only child for nine years and he liked it that way. As the only child of the family, he was the center of attention to both his father and mother, who were always showering him with gifts and special treats. Juanito, however, began to question if this special treatment from his parents would continue after the birth of his baby sister, Teresita. At first, Juanito had been thrilled at the prospect of being an older brother, but the more he thought about it, the less he liked it. Juanito's worst fears were proven to be true shortly after the arrival of his baby sister. Everyone would always make a fuss over how pretty little Teresita was.

"She is so beautiful!" commented all the relatives.

"Beautiful?" questioned Juanito. How could anybody even think that a baby as ugly as little Teresita could be beautiful? The baby whose face he saw on the jars of baby food that his mother bought, with its rounded pink cheeks and bright oval-shaped eyes, was a pretty baby. Its skin was not all wrinkled like a prune the way that Teresita's was. What was even worse, all Teresita ever seemed to do was cry and poop in her diaper! And Juanito was none too excited about having to take his little sister's "personal business" to the garbage can outside the house. It was during one of these trips that Juanito began to hear voices talking in his head.

"She's ruining everything," the voices would declare. "Things were so much better before she came along. I bet your parents don't even love you anymore. They love little Teresita now!"

The boy was heartbroken at what the voices were telling him. Did his parents truly not love him anymore? Had little Teresita replaced him in their hearts? Juanito began to hate his little sister and he took advantage of every opportunity he got to be mean to her. The voices kept urging him on.

"Go ahead, do it, steal and hide all her toys," they encouraged.

One day they asked him to do the unthinkable.

"We can make her go away, you know," the voices explained. "We can get rid of little Teresita for you. With her gone, you will once again be your mother and father's favorite!"

Juanito listened attentively to every word the voices said.

"All you have to do is say yes," the voices declared. "Say yes and you can consider it done."

Juanito took a deep breath and then uttered the word, "Yes!"

Juanito then heard his mother scream from inside the

baby's room! When he ran in to see what was happening, Juanito saw that his mother was on the floor crying and that his father was banging his fists on the wall.

"*Duende*s," his mother cried out. "*Duende*s with green skin and glowing-red eyes came out from the walls and took your baby sister!"

🌿 🌿 🌿

Ten years later, a nineteen-year-old named Juanito is awakened from his sleep by sudden scratching sounds on the walls.

"Who's there?" he asks, but he is only greeted by silence. Closing his eyes, the young man goes back to sleep, but is soon awakened by the scratching noises, this time on the floor.

"What's going on here?" he cries out as he turns on the lamp next to his bed. When light fills the room, Juanito sees that it is empty except for himself.

Going back to sleep, he is awakened yet a third time by the soft murmur of a child's voice.

"Juanito, are you awake?" the voice asks.

Juanito, very much startled, jumps out of his bed. Surrounded by the darkness of his room, Juanito sees what appears to be the black silhouette of a small child standing on his bed.

Quickly turning on the lamp next to his bed, Juanito sees a short, green-skinned and red-eyed girl in pigtails staring back at him.

"What are you?" he cries out very afraid, but the green-skinned and red-eyed girl only stares at him and smiles.

"It took me a while to find you, but I never stopped looking. I knew that I would find you someday," says the girl. "It's me, Juanito, your baby sister Teresita. You know, the one you gave away to the *duendes!* Look at what they did to me," she declares. "Look at what they did to me!"

Terrified, Juanito can only stare at his sister who has become a *duende*.

"But now that I found you, big brother," she replies, showing him her talon-like claws, "now that I found you, I intend to play with you!"

Juanito screams in terror, and is never seen again.

Las Lechuzas versus El Curandero

A long, white beard adorning his aged face, the old *curandero*, medicine man, was sitting outside his one-room shack when he saw the patrol car pulling up. The elder, it was said by the locals, was a great healer who accepted no credit for the good work that he did. Instead, he always said that he healed people for the greater glory of God. The *curandero* was known far and wide for his ability to help people. But he faced many dangers in his life, mostly from multiple battles with *lechuzas*, bewitched owls. Dozens of stories circulated of how *lechuzas* came to test their powers against this old *curandero*, only to be sent back home humiliated and with their feathers ruffled.

Sheriff Martínez had never been one to believe in these stories, which he referred to as "silly superstitions," but he was truly at a loss to explain a sudden rash of child disappearances. In the last three months, more than a dozen children had turned up missing, several stolen right from their cribs. The public was rightfully demanding action from him, but he did not have one single plausible clue to work with. Being a rational man, he had not believed any of the local rumors that claimed the child abductions were the

work of *lechuzas*.

Sheriff Martínez knew from the stories of his youth that a *lechuza* was a witch who took the form of a giant white owl. These evil beings were said to travel in packs, preying on children left unattended by neglectful parents. He remembered how when growing up, if a child ever turned up missing from its crib, the blame had been placed squarely on the *lechuzas*. The stolen children, it was said, were brainwashed and trained in the arts of black magic. The most evil of the children would eventually be turned into *lechuzas* to ensure the survival of their evil clan.

Sheriff Martínez had always considered these stories to be ridiculous, but the sudden disappearance of his six-year-old daughter had led him to seek avenues of help that he would not have imagined using before. The sheriff's daughter had in fact been stolen from her bed as she slept. The only thing he had found that came close to a clue were giant white feathers left on her bed, the same feathers that had been found at all the other crime scenes.

"You are a good man," said the *curandero* upon meeting Sheriff Martínez, "an honest and just man, I can tell, but you have no faith. Still, God has seen fit to bring you to me for a reason. Perhaps we will find both your daughter and your faith today." That having been said, the aged *curandero* got into the passenger seat of the patrol car, and they both drove away.

"I know I have to put a stop to it," said the *curandero*. "The minute I heard about the child abductions I was suspicious, but when you mentioned the white feathers found on your daughter's bed, I had no doubt in my mind. I knew at that point that no human being could be behind such horrendous abductions."

"How will we find them?" asked Sheriff Martínez hesitantly. "I mean, how does one find a *lechuza*, and is there even such a thing?"

"Faith," said the old *curandero* smiling. "You just have to have a little bit of faith."

The old *curandero* closed his eyes and began to pray. After a while, it seemed to Sheriff Martínez as if the *curandero* was lost in a trance, muttering prayers under his breath and speaking in tongues. The *curandero*'s eyes suddenly drew open, and he cried out one word: "¡*Calaveras!*"

Moments later the old *curandero* and Sheriff Martínez were pulling up in front of an old abandoned warehouse on Calaveras Street, Street of Skulls. After calling for backup, the old *curandero* and Sheriff Martínez made their way into the warehouse. Sheriff Martínez was shocked to find eight very old-looking women burning black candles and chanting what sounded like demonic verses. As startling as these images were to Sheriff Martínez, they were not as appalling as the gruesome scene of children being kept in cages, as if they were animals. His own daughter was among them!

The *curandero* walked out to the women and interrupted their ceremony by reciting the Lord's Prayer as he tied knots on a rope made of rawhide, one for each prayer he completed. The old women, hissing and hooting as if they were owls, seemed eager to pounce on the old *curandero*, but to Sheriff Martínez it seemed as if some invisible force was holding them at bay. As Sheriff Martínez quickly freed and gathered the children, the *curandero* completed his eighth and final prayer. Then he began untying the knots, and as he did this, each woman began to faint, falling helplessly to the ground!

Sheriff Martínez was truly stunned by what he had just seen. "God's power must truly be great," he whispered to himself as he blessed himself with the sign of the cross.

Once the police backup arrived, all eight women were placed inside three patrol cars and sent on their way to jail. En route to the police station, however, all eight women somehow managed to escape from police custody.

"It was the strangest thing," commented a police deputy to Sheriff Martínez later that day. "When we got to police headquarters, all eight women were gone. In their place were giant white owls that flew out and escaped as soon as we opened the doors of the patrol cars!"

All of the children were returned to their grateful parents, and Sheriff Martínez was happily reunited with his daughter. But the police were never able to find any of the eight fugitives. Thankfully, the rash of child disappearances stopped at that point, but who knew for how long.

Lechuza Lady

"The story of *Lechuza* Lady is nothing but a bunch of lies!" declared Don Fidencio, who was not convinced by his wife's argument that he should not go out drinking that night.

"The story is true," responded Don Fidencio's wife, Cristina, "and I pray that you never have to find out just how true it is."

Don Fidencio laughed out loud and told her not to wait up for him. Moments later, he made his way out of the house and began his walk down the half mile of winding dirt road that led to El Rincón del Diablo bar. Don Fidencio had heard many stories of *Lechuza* Lady. He knew all too well of the woman who had become a large white owl in order to avenge the death of her son at the hands of a drunken driver. After learning of her son's death, it was said that the woman had cursed the infamous bar district in which El Rincón del Diablo existed. She had taken to preying on its drunks to avenge her son's death. Don Fidencio considered these stories to be pure nonsense. Besides, it would take a lot more than an overgrown bird to scare him away.

That night, Don Fidencio drank even more than usual, and at two o'clock in the morning, when the bar closed down, he began to walk home. Weaving from side to side, Don Fidencio struggled to stay on the path of the winding dirt road that would lead him back to his house. As he turned on a corner, he heard the sound of a voice calling out to him in the wind.

"*¡Borracho!*" the voice declared, calling Don Fidencio a drunk.

"What?" questioned Don Fidencio, who looked around but saw no one.

"*¡Borracho!*" the voice declared once again, but Don Fidencio still saw no one.

Don Fidencio was beginning to get scared now. He could even feel the hairs on the back of his neck begin to rise up. He tried to walk as fast as he possibly could, but he was so drunk that the faster he tried to walk, the more he stumbled and fell to the ground!

"*¡Borracho!*" the voice called out to him one more time. That is when a giant white owl sprung from one of the trees and attacked Don Fidencio!

"*¡Borracho! ¡Borracho!*" the *lechuza* cried out as its talons tore into his face, and he tried to struggle with the feathered fury. Falling down to the ground, Don Fidencio began to crawl on all fours like a scolded dog in an attempt to get away from the attacking bird. All this time he kept hearing the *lechuza* cry out, "*¡Borracho! ¡Borracho!*"

Don Fidencio finally made it home, and when he turned

around to look back, he saw that the *lechuza* was gone. In its place was a white-haired woman pointing an accusing finger at him. She cried out, "*¡Borracho!*" before disappearing in a puff of smoke.

Don Fidencio never drank again.

The Onion House

During the Great Depression in the 1930s, many people lost their jobs. This is the story of a young man and his family who could not pay their bills, and as a result, they lost their home and had to live in the streets. A kind old man who felt sorry for the family told them that he had an extra house that he never used, and that they were welcomed to use it.

The house was very old and looked like it was falling apart, but to the family it was better than living in the streets. The proud young man humbly agreed to have his family stay in the house, but said that he did not want to stay at the house without paying some manner of rent. The old man said that he understood, and suggested that the family could sell produce outside the house. The old man owned a produce store on the south side of the city and had always wanted to open a second location on the north side. He said that they could share the profits, once he recovered the money he invested in growing the produce.

Over a short period of time, the plan worked well and the business was soon thriving. The house came to be known as "The Onion House" because of the huge and

tasty onions the family sold. The young man worked very hard and soon was making enough money to pay rent to the old man and to buy food and clothes for his family.

All seemed well until the day that the old man grew ill and died. The old man's son, who had inherited the house, was nothing like his kind father. He was a cruel and selfish man who took delight in the misfortunes of others. As the new landlord of the house, he began to demand more and more money from the family each month. If they refused to meet his demands, he threatened to have them evicted. The house was very old before the young man and his family had moved in, and it was soon in need of major repairs when the top floor of the house began to rot away.

"You should be happy that you at least have a roof over your heads!" declared the greedy son who refused to do any of the needed repairs.

The top floor of the house grew weaker and weaker until, one day, the whole second level came crashing down, killing the entire family. Months later, the greedy son was still hoping to make some money from the old house. He took out a very big loan from a bank to repair it thinking that he could make a profit by selling it. Perhaps it was a form of divine punishment for having been so cruel to the family that had lived and died in the house, but the greedy son was never able to sell or even rent the house. Countless people came to see the house that was for sale, but left moments later, screaming that the house was haunted by ghosts! They claimed that a whole family of ghosts could be seen lurking about the house at all hours of the day.

The loss of the money he had invested in the repairs financially ruined the greedy son, who soon found himself homeless and living in the streets. To this very day, "The Onion House" remains unsold.

La Llorona

There was once a beautiful but very poor Mexican girl named Cristina who fell in love with a handsome young man named Héctor Ortega. He was the son of a wealthy *caballero* who owned the lands where the girl's family grew its crops. The handsome but cruel young man played with young Cristina's feelings, promising to marry her if she would give her love to him. This was a promise that the son of the wealthy landowner had never planned on keeping. The man that Cristina believed would be her one true love soon abandoned her, choosing to marry instead a woman he considered to be more fitting to his social status. The only two things that he would leave Cristina would be the two twin boys she had given birth to during their passionate love affair.

Perhaps as a punishment from God for the way he had treated Cristina, the woman that Héctor had taken as his bride proved to be barren, and would be unable to give him a son to continue his family name. Just as he was about to reach the point of despair, the young man remembered the two boys he had fathered with Cristina.

The cruel young man told Cristina that he realized what a horrible mistake he had made and promised that he would divorce the woman he had married and take Cristina as his bride instead. Héctor, however, had no intention of divorcing his wife or marrying Cristina. He planned on taking the two boys and leaving Cristina behind. Cristina became suspicious of him when he insisted that he take the two boys first and then return for her later that evening. Cristina ran out of the house, carrying her two boys with her. The young man gave chase and cornered Cristina near the river that ran close to her house. The river was running fast that day, overflowing its banks from the recent rains. Left with nowhere to run, Cristina began to back herself into the river with the two boys held tightly to her chest. The young man followed her into the water and got closer and closer with each step. The closer Héctor got, the deeper Cristina and her boys went into the water. Cristina suddenly lost her footing and fell into the raging water whose current carried her and her boys away, drowning all three!

The story of Cristina, however, was not to end there. The woman was so distraught over the death of her children that her soul could not rest. A few moments after seeing Cristina and his sons drowned by the current, Héctor saw a white silhouette rise inches above the water and begin to walk toward him.

"Where are my children?" the ghostly apparition asked.

Héctor became so frightened by what he saw that he died on the spot, the victim of a sudden heart attack induced by fear!

Now, years later, it is said that the spirit of Cristina is still searching for her children. The stories tell that if you listen at night, you can hear her cries of lament in the howling wind. That is why people call her "La Llorona," which in Spanish means "The Crying Woman." Each evening she wanders along rivers and streams crying, *"¡Ay, mis hijos!,"* "Oh, my children!," pleading with the dark waters.

Another Version of La Llorona Story

Cristina was a woman of striking beauty. Her crystalline blue eyes were as calm and soothing as the sun shining over the Rio Grande River at sunset. Like all pretty young girls, Cristina had many suitors. Day after day, they sought her hand in marriage. Of all of them, it would be a tall and strapping bronze-skinned young lad with woolly black hair named Héctor Ortega who would find the right words to capture her heart. Héctor was new to the region, a recent arrival from Mexico who had come to Texas with hopes of a better life.

After a brief courting period, as was the custom, Cristina and Héctor were married. Less than a year later, Cristina gave birth to twins, one boy and one girl. All was not happiness for the young couple, however, as Héctor had come to Texas at the time when "Los Rinches," the Texas Rangers, were running rough over the land. Cutthroats and murderers had overrun the Southwest, and Mexican bandits were known for stealing both cattle and horses. The governor of Texas had sent Rangers to the region to restore order by any means necessary. The Rangers were cruel and sadistic in their quest to bring order and justice to the land.

Many innocent Mexican farmers were wrongfully accused and executed for crimes that they did not commit. The Rangers eventually achieved their objective and brought order to the region, but their success had come at the expense of innocent ranchers who had been mistaken for cutthroats and cattle rustlers. One of those innocent victims was Héctor Ortega, Cristina's husband.

Grief stricken, Cristina changed after the murder of her husband. The fact that she still had her twins did not seem to matter to her. Cristina's children grew up running around in tattered clothes, even having to beg in the streets for food. Cristina did not seem to care. She only wished to be left alone with the memories of the only man she had ever loved. Cristina resolved at that point that she had to leave the Rio Grande Valley. Then and there she swore to abandon that corner of the world that had taken so much from her.

Shortly after making her decision it came to pass that she met an elderly man from Monterrey named Don Ismael Sánchez. The man had an elegant swagger about him. He was considerably older than Cristina was, three times her age, in fact. In Don Ismael Sánchez, Cristina saw the opportunity she had been looking for to escape the Rio Grande Valley. Don Ismael had never married before and had no children, so she thought that she could endure being married to the old gizzard for a few years before inheriting all of his great wealth.

After a brief courtship, Cristina accepted the old man's marriage proposal and invitation to move with him to Mon-

terrey. But Cristina had hidden from him the fact that she had two children. She knew the old man had no use for children and did not want any. He always said that he was too old to be chasing after brats and, quite frankly, was annoyed by their noisy presence. That posed a problem for Cristina, but she would not have her plans altered. This was her one opportunity to escape the poverty she lived in. Cristina would not allow anyone, not even her own children, to stand in her way. So she decided then and there that she would murder them. It was a gruesome idea, as evil as if the Devil himself had conjured up the plan. Cristina resolved not to dwell on her decision, and that night she greeted her children with open arms.

It is often said that cold blood ran through the veins of Cristina on the night she committed the murders. Given her careful planning, one would be inclined to believe so. Cristina first gathered herbs that were known to induce sleep and mixed them into two cups of warm goat's milk. She spoke to her children about moving to Monterrey together. Everything would be perfect there, she assured them. Cristina packed her bags and prepared for her trip as her children finished drinking the goat's milk. Cristina assured them that upon their arrival in Monterrey, they would go to one of those fancy clothing stores that were found in big cities. She would buy them clothes and shoes, just like the ones worn by wealthy kids. Her children fell asleep listening to her empty promises.

That night, under the cloak of darkness, Cristina

wrapped her children in blankets and then hurriedly carried them both to the Rio Grande River. She tied her children with a rope to ensure that they would not free themselves, and then she placed heavy rocks in each bundle. Without so much as shedding a tear of guilt, Cristina tossed her children into the raging waters. Mercifully, the herbs that had induced their sleep had also prevented the two children from feeling anything as their tiny lungs began to fill with water.

Cristina left the valley for Monterrey the very next morning and, shortly thereafter, married the old man. True to her promise, she never returned to the Rio Grande Valley. Her husband would die a year later in a tragic accident that saw him fall down a flight of stairs. Cristina inherited the old man's money, his lands, and everything else. She lived a life of luxury until she died of old age.

After her death, Cristina found herself having to stand before God and be judged for her sins. God's eyes had seemed like accusing orbs of fire to Cristina. Did God know what she had done? she wondered.

"Where are your children?" God asked.

Cristina did not answer. She knew that God hated a sinner, and the murder of innocent children was surely the worst sin of all.

"Where are your children?" God asked again.

Cristina was speechless. What excuse could she possibly give to justify her actions?

God asked the question a third and final time, his voice

echoing like raging thunder, "Where are your children?"

"I have no children," she answered, her voice an almost mute whisper.

"Liar!" God declared angrily.

Cristina broke into loud wails as her eyes began filling with tears.

Raising his right hand, God pointed an accusing finger at Cristina and addressed her by her new name.

"¡Llorona!"

God then condemned Cristina's soul never to know rest, to walk the earth forever as a ghost who would be shunned by all. "Llorona," God had called her, for she was condemned to cry out each evening, "Oh, my children!" as she searched for them. It is the name by which she is still known.

Many are the legends that tell of how her troubled spirit still wanders the earth, looking for the bodies of her dead children. She is still out there, they say, still searching, still crying out, *"¡Ay, mis hijos!"*

The Vanishing Hitchhiker

Driving his Chevy truck down old Highway 83 on his way to a night of dancing and fun at El Bocasios Nightclub, Eduardo García noticed that a young girl dressed in a white party dress was standing alongside the road. Now, Eduardo was not in the habit of picking up hitchhikers, but being the Good Samaritan that he was, he decided to stop and see if the girl was in need of help. For all he knew, the girl's car might have broken down.

"Hey, need some help?" Eduardo called out as he pulled up next to the young lady. "Can I help or offer you a ride or something?" he asked.

"By any chance, are you going to the dance?" the girl asked.

"Why, yes," said an elated Eduardo. "Do you want to go with me?" he asked. "I'm an okay dancer, and I have no date." The young girl smiled and then nodded her head in a gesture of yes.

At the dance, Eduardo had the best time of his life dancing with the young beauty whose name was Cecilia Cantú. He could not believe how lucky he was to have found her. Driving back home after the dance, the girl told Eduardo that she had gone to the dance against her father's wishes.

Her father, she said, had felt that she was far too young to be going to dances on her own, and he was too tired from working all day to be her chaperone. The girl, however, said that she had felt an urge to be at the dance tonight. She could feel it in her heart that if she did not go, she would never meet the one true love of her life.

"I felt the same way!" said Eduardo. "I rarely go to dances because, as I am sure you noticed, I have two left feet when it comes to rhythm. But something told me that I just had to go tonight. I knew that if I didn't go, I would regret it forever. The minute I laid my eyes on you, Cecilia, I knew that I had found the one true love of my life."

Those words having been said, Eduardo and the girl kissed. Later that night, Eduardo dropped her off at the exact same spot he had found her.

"I'll be fine," the girl said to Eduardo, who was hesitant to drop her off on the side of the road. "I live one block down on the other side of the train tracks in a pink house, the only pink house on the whole block," she told him. "Besides, your car's headlights might wake up my father, and if that happens, then we would both be in real trouble."

"Well, here, take my coat; it will keep you warm," said Eduardo, noticing for the first time just how cold the night had suddenly gotten. As he placed his coat on her shoulders, Eduardo kissed Cecilia good night. She in turn told Eduardo that she would love him forever. She walked away and disappeared into the shadows.

❧ ❧ ❧

"What do you mean, she's dead?" questioned Eduardo, whose joy at his newfound love had suddenly been cut short. He had shown up the very next day at Cecilia's home to pick up his coat, only to be told that the girl he had fallen in love with the night before had been dead for over five years!

"She was killed five years ago," the girl's father said. "She had really wanted to go to a dance at El Bocasios Night Club, but I was too tired to take her. When I went to sleep that night, she climbed out her window and made her way to old Highway 83 in hopes of catching a ride to the nightclub. A drunken driver ran her down," he explained. "She might have lived, had she been taken to a hospital right away, but the driver that hit her didn't even bother to stop and call for help!"

Eduardo García, who was shocked by the man's revelation, refused to believe his story. Then, the old man took him to the cemetery where his daughter was buried. It was there that Eduardo found his coat neatly folded on top of Cecilia's tombstone! Inside his coat pocket was a note that read: "Eduardo, I will always love you, Cecilia."

Eduardo had fallen in love with a ghost!

🌿 🌿 🌿

To this very day it is said that Eduardo García parks his car by old Highway 83 in hopes of reuniting with his one true love.

The Severed Hand's Revenge

Luis Murrieta didn't know it at the time, but he was the chosen scapegoat for the two Texas Rangers who had been stealing and selling cattle illegally across the border to make extra money. When their scheme was discovered, they needed to place the blame on someone, and poor Luis Murrieta, who did not speak a word of English, was the perfect victim for their cruel plan. By framing Murrieta, not only would they be able to keep their scheme a secret, but they could even lay claim to having captured a "vile Mexican cattle rustler."

Luis Murrieta justly protested his innocence, but he knew that there was no way the two Texas Rangers would ever allow him to go free. The night before he was to be hanged, he attempted a daring prison escape that ended badly when it was discovered by the two rangers. During the struggle, Luis struck one of the rangers in the face. This angered the ranger, and once Luis was subdued, the ranger used a machete to sever the hand that had dared to strike his face!

The miscarriage of justice was swift in the days of the rangers, and, before sunrise, Luis Murrieta was hanging

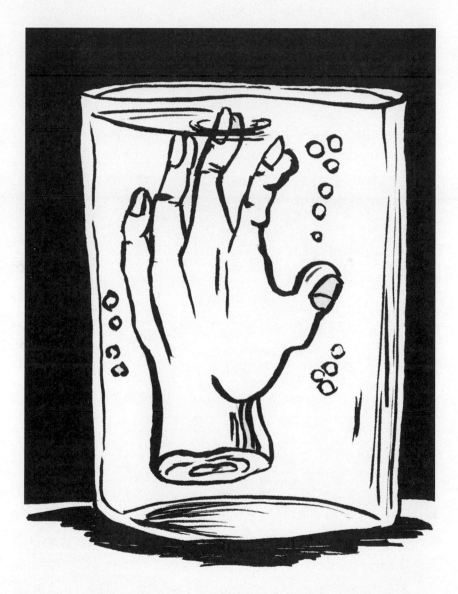

lifeless from a tree. One of the rangers had even kept Murrieta's severed hand in a glass jar filled with formaldehyde; it was to be a macabre trophy. Both rangers had believed themselves to have gotten away with blatant murder, but, six nights later, they would both be proven wrong.

Luis Murrieta would have his revenge, or at least his severed left hand would. The ranger that had kept Murrieta's hand as a souvenir was found dead at a local hotel room, a victim of strangulation! Written in blood on the mirror was one word: *"inocente,"* which in Spanish means "innocent."

The surviving ranger could not find a single clue as to who had murdered his friend. Five nights later as he went to sleep, the ranger heard scratching sounds, as if something was dragging itself across the bedroom floor. He immediately jumped out of bed, but saw nothing in the room. He went back to sleep, but was awakened when he felt something pulling at his bedsheets. Immediately he drew out his revolver, but found nothing to aim his revolver to! It was at this point that he noticed that something had been written on the wall. It was the word *"¡inocente!"* The ranger suddenly felt a viselike grip tighten around his throat! It was the putrid and decaying hand that had belonged to Luis Murrieta! The ranger helplessly felt its bony fingers tightening themselves more and more around his throat!

The ranger was found dead the next morning, another victim of strangulation.

The Haunted Train Tracks of San Antonio

I t was during a storm about thirty years ago when a school-bus driver was running way behind schedule. He came across the old train tracks that run near the Missions District in the city of San Antonio. He was in such a hurry to finish his route and get rid of all the noisy kids he was taking home that he chose to speed across the old train tracks without first coming to a complete stop. Had he stopped, he might have seen that a speeding train was only a few feet away! Before the startled bus driver could react, the train plowed into the bus, killing the driver and every child on board!

The news of the tragic accident swept across the old neighborhood. Seemingly every family that lived there had lost a son or a daughter that day. One year later, an old man's car stalled on the same train tracks. The old man had started to gripe and complain about having to get out of his car and push, when he heard the alarming sound of a train whistle!

"*¡Dios mío!*" the old man cried out as he saw a rapidly advancing train heading right for him! He quickly turned the key in the ignition, but the car still would not start! The old man then gripped the car's door handle, but it too

would not turn or open. "I knew I should have fixed it," the old man cried out and began struggling to climb out of his seat and exit through the passenger door. When he realized that he was not going to make it, the old man began hollering out in fear and closed his eyes as he waited for the impact that would definitely kill him. That is when his car suddenly began to jerk forward and roll off the tracks. It was as if some invisible force had actually pushed the car up and over the train tracks. As the old man's car rolled down the hill, it narrowly avoided being hit by the speeding train that flew by with less than an inch to spare!

The old man stumbled out from the passenger's door and fell to the ground, gasping for air. What had just happened? he wondered. What had pushed his car off the train tracks? Then the answer came to him, for standing on the train tracks he saw more than a dozen children, children who seemed to disappear in the blink of an eye!

🍃 🍃 🍃

"It's the ghosts of the children," declared the old man to the local folks when explaining what had happened. "It's the ghosts of the children who saved my life," he assured the crowd that had gathered to listen to his story. "They didn't want me to suffer their same tragic fate."

Nobody in the neighborhood believed him, of course. They all felt that the old man had just gotten lucky. They assured him that there had to be a rational explanation for what had happened. The old man, however, did not agree.

"If there is a rational explanation, I sure would like to

hear it, especially when it comes to explaining how *these* got here," he declared and then pointed to his car's rear bumper. The crowd quickly gathered around the vehicle, their eyes opening wide with a combination of awe and horror. The car's rear bumper was covered with dozens of children's handprints, the handprints of the children who had died a year earlier!

The Handsome Stranger

L uz was having the time of her life as she danced the night away at El Bocasios Nightclub. With her honey-colored skin, lime-colored eyes, and skintight red satin dress, Luz Escobedo was easily the most beautiful girl at the club that night. Suitor after suitor lined up from one end of the dance hall to the other, each waiting impatiently for his turn to dance with the beautiful Luz. They all hoped to be the lucky one, to be the fortunate soul that would steal her heart.

"She is so lucky to be so beautiful," commented Mirasol Solís, who was one of the many girls in attendance that had lined up against the opposite wall, waiting to be asked to dance.

"I don't like her," replied her friend Estela Rodríguez, who had been waiting unsuccessfully for more than an hour to be asked to dance. "I think she is just so conceited because guys like her so much," said Estela.

"She's not the same Luz we knew back in junior high when we were kids," commented Estela. "You have to accept the fact that Luz has changed, Mirasol. When was the last time she even said 'hi' to us?"

Mirasol, Luz, and Estela had been friends in junior high; best friends, in fact. That changed, however, when Luz began to blossom into a beautiful young woman and Mirasol and Estela did not. Everybody liked Mirasol and Estela, but not in the same way they liked Luz, at least not the way guys did.

"It's not her fault," said Mirasol.

"Right," commented Estela sarcastically. "I will never forgive her for what she did to my brother Lalo. She shouldn't have played with his feelings the way she did. She made Lalo think that she really loved him, and then after two years, she had the nerve to tell him that she wanted to break up with him and that they should just be friends. She left my brother because she wanted to date a bunch of other guys. What she did wasn't right, Mirasol, and you know it! My brother was a good guy and didn't deserve to be treated like that. That's why he killed himself, you know, because he couldn't bear what she had done to him. But it will come back to haunt her someday. Her kind always gets it in the end."

Everybody knew everybody at El Bocasios Nightclub, so when a handsome stranger suddenly showed up, it became the talk of the night. Who was he? Where did he come from? Was he alone or with someone? The stranger had an olive-oil color to his skin and wore a white western shirt that was neatly tucked into his black wrangler jeans. All of this, along with the jumbo-sized Texas-shaped belt buckle strapped around his waist, truly made the stranger a peculiar sight. Everyone watched silently as he cut line and made his way toward Luz, the heels of his rattlesnake-skin boots scraping against the wooden dance floor. One of the guys at the front had begun to complain about the handsome stranger cutting in line, but fell silent after the stranger cast him a quick and menacing glare. Luz could not help but stare at the facial features of this handsome stranger, who in turn smiled and flashed his baby-blue eyes at her from underneath his black Stetson hat.

"Want to dance?" the stranger asked in a soft but confident whisper.

He then took Luz by the arm and together they began to burn up the dance floor! The handsome stranger was more than just a good dancer; he was the best dancer anyone had ever seen at El Bocasios Nightclub. He knew every step, every twist, and every turn that there was to know when it came to dancing. What's more, he never seemed to tire or even break into a sweat. Even Luz, who had always fancied herself a dance expert, could hardly keep up with him.

"You've been a bad girl, Luz," said the stranger, whispering in her ear during a particularly slow ballad. "A very bad girl, indeed. Do you know what happens to bad girls?"

Luz smiled, believing the stranger to be flirting with her. "What happens to bad girls?" she asked.

"I can't tell you. I'll have to show you," said the stranger. "Do you want me to show you?"

"Yes, I want you to show me," whispered Luz in the stranger's ear. It was then that, by chance, Luz happened to

look down at the handsome stranger's feet and notice that his feet seemed to be changing right before her eyes! One minute they looked like a pair of rapidly moving snakeskin boots, but the next she could swear that they looked as if one was the foot of a chicken and the other that of a goat! Horrified, Luz looked up at the stranger and saw that his handsome face seemed to be changing too! The horned and red facial features of the Devil were replacing his once handsome appearance! A giant ring of fire suddenly erupted around the dance floor and flames began to engulf El Bocasios Nightclub. People ran for the exit, trampling each other as they tried desperately to escape from the rapidly burning building.

"Nothing will save El Bocasios tonight," cried out the stranger. "And nothing will save Luz Escobedo either!" The whole building then crumbled down to the ground, burying dozens of people!

Firefighters would later recover the burnt remains of all the victims, Luz Escobedo among them. Her body had been burned to a crisp! But the handsome stranger's body was never found. All that remained as proof that he had ever been at El Bocasios Nightclub were the charred remains of his black Stetson hat.

The Burning Ghost

"It happened in 1979," declares the man sitting at the bar, who is as thin as a toothpick. "I still remember it like it was yesterday."

"Remember what, *compadre?*" questions his beer-drinking buddy, a rather obese and unshaven man.

"The ghost story, *compadrito,*" he declares. "That's when the story first started."

"Ghost story?" the man questions. "What ghost?"

"The ghost that haunts this bar," declares the thin man. "Didn't you know about it? Years ago, a Mexican girl named Zulema was working as a barmaid here and had been living in a small room at the back of the bar. One night, a man got way too drunk and started making amorous advances at Zulema, advances that the young girl didn't much appreciate. It was then that the bar owner, a rather large man, kicked the guy out for being disrespectful to the girl. The angry drunk swore that he would have his revenge on both Zulema and the bar owner. Later that same night, he returned after the bar had closed down and set fire to the place. The young girl, who had been fast asleep in the back room at the time, found herself trapped inside the

bar and was burned alive!"

"Did that really happen, *compadre?*"

"It sure did," said the bartender, suddenly joining in on the conversation. "I bought this bar ten years ago from the original owner and reopened it after I painted over its burnt walls with a fresh coat of paint. Things may seem pretty normal now, but for a long time a lot of my patrons claimed to see the ghost of the girl that was burned alive. They said that they could hear her scream as if she were still being burned alive today!"

"You guys are just trying to scare me," declared the obese and unshaven man, "but I'm not falling for it." The man rose from the stool he was sitting on and made his way to the men's restroom. After drinking seven consecutive beers, Mother Nature had begun to make her call.

"That's the dumbest story I have ever heard," muttered the man as he pulled down his pants and let nature take its course. "There are no such things as ghosts!"

"Help!" a voice suddenly cried out in a soft whisper. Just then the lights went out, leaving the men's room pitch black!

"Who's out there?" asked the startled man.

"Help me, I'm burning!" the voice cried out once again, sounding closer this time.

"Cut it out, guys," the man called out, convinced that his buddies were playing a joke. "No way am I letting you guys scare me. Everybody knows there is no such thing as a ghost!"

"Help me, I'm being burned alive!" the voice called out loudly one last time before a burning woman suddenly appeared in front of the man!

"Help me!" the burning spirit cried out as it reached out toward him, her hands engulfed in flames!

"*¡Dios mío!*" the man cried out as he stood up from where he was sitting and ran out of the men's room hollering for help. Scared out of his wits, the man ran hysterically around the room twice before he finally ran out of the bar, without even bothering to pick up his pants!

The Donkey Lady

It was already getting dark by the time Antonio Barrientos finally left his cousin Lupe's birthday party and began his seventy-mile drive down the stretch of old road known as Highway 107. He had planned to leave the party early, but could not seem to break away from the fun of being with family and friends. He knew that it would be a good solid hour before he got to his dorm room at college. Antonio did not like going down Highway 107 at night because, with the exception of one small convenience store, it was deserted until he reached the city of Edinburg, Texas. Antonio, however, knew that he really needed to get some rest before his big chemistry test Monday morning, and it would be easier and less stressful for him to drive for one hour at night than to fight the morning traffic commute, which could truly be horrendous.

"It sure is dark," commented Antonio to himself, "dark and scary."

No sooner had Antonio said those words than he caught sight of a lady walking alongside the highway.

"What's anybody doing walking out here in the middle of nowhere this late at night?" he wondered. Antonio

decided to stop and see if the lady needed help. Perhaps her car had stalled.

"Hey, do you need any help?" asked Antonio as he pulled up beside the lady.

She gave no response.

"It's okay," said Antonio, "I'm not going to hurt you, I just want to help," he assured her.

The lady then began to move closer to Antonio's car, her head bowed down as if to conceal her face.

"Look, lady, I'm sorry if I scared you," Antonio began to say, but cut his sentence short when the lady looked up at him. Her face was the face of a donkey!

The Donkey Lady gave out a loud and horrendous wail just as Antonio slammed his foot down on the gas pedal! As he sped away, Antonio turned to look at his rearview mirror. "She's right behind me!" he cried out as he noticed that the Donkey Lady had dropped down on all fours and was now giving chase.

Galloping as if she were a horse, the Donkey Lady seemed to be moving faster and faster and, as impossible as it seemed, was catching up to him! It did not seem to matter how fast Antonio was driving, the Donkey Lady just kept drawing nearer and nearer. Antonio caught sight of the convenience store that was coming up about a mile down the road and began to speed up in an attempt to reach the store and ask the clerk for help. Just then, Antonio glanced to his side and saw that the Donkey Lady was running right beside his car! She bared her teeth at him in a menacing grin and then her eyes began to smolder like red-hot ambers!

"Leave me alone!" cried out Antonio. "Why won't you just leave me alone?! I was only trying to help!"

At that moment, Antonio noticed that the Donkey Lady seemed to be slowing down. The closer he got to the lights of the convenience store, the more the Donkey Lady fell behind. Just as Antonio finished pulling into the convenience store parking lot, the Donkey Lady slowly disappeared into thin air.

Never again did Antonio Barrientos drive down Highway 107 so late at night.

El Big Bird

"**E**l Big Bird is real," declared Don Cipriano to the group of ten-year-olds gathered at his front porch to listen to his latest *cucuy* story. Children loved to listen to Don Cipriano spin his tales of wonderment. Today, he had chosen as his subject what could easily be the scariest *cucuy* of them all, El Big Bird.

"Some people want you to believe that El Big Bird is a lie, that it doesn't exist, but it does," declared Don Cipriano. "It wasn't that long ago that El Big Bird struck right here, in your own hometown!"

"El Big Bird was here?" questioned Simón, one of the children listening to the story.

"Oh, yes," declared Don Cipriano. "It was down by El Canal del Diablo, The Devil's Creek, where cows are known to graze often. I saw it with my very own eyes," he declared, opening them wide like shutters that had been suddenly drawn open. "I was walking down the creek when I saw a shadow the size of a small plane pass over me. Looking up, I saw a giant gray bird with leather wings like those flying dinosaurs used to have. 'El Big Bird!' I cried out, and ran to hide behind some rocks. Then I watched as

it scooped up the biggest and fattest cows in the herd with its beak! El Big Bird swallowed each and every cow in one mighty gulp! Once he satisfied his hunger, he flew away!"

"Wow," declared little Martín, Simón's baby brother, "you mean that El Big Bird lives near El Canal del Diablo?"

"That's where I saw him last," answered Don Cipriano.

The children started to say that they wanted to hear another story, but Don Cipriano warned that it was starting to get dark and that they should go home.

"You don't want your parents getting worried now."

The disappointed children whined for a while, but then reluctantly agreed that Don Cipriano was right.

"Be careful now," he warned them. "Don't let El Big Bird get you!"

The children silently went their separate ways, all frightened by the journey home that lay before them. Most of the children lived only half a mile away, except for Simón and Martín, who had to walk a full two miles down El Canal del Diablo to get home, the same canal where Don Cipriano had supposedly seen El Big Bird!

"There is no Big Bird," Simón kept repeating as he and Martín ran quickly down the stretch of dirt road that ran parallel to El Canal del Diablo. "It is just a story, and a dumb story, at that."

"Are you sure?" asked Martín, who was not convinced by his older brother's words.

"Yes, I'm sure," declared Simón. "Remember what

Daddy told us about Don Cipriano being a good liar?"

"Yes," Martín agreed, "he said that's the reason why he is so good at telling scary stories that just aren't true."

SSSWWOOOSSSHHHH!

"What was that?" questioned Martín, startled by the sudden burst of wind that had just blown over their heads.

"It was probably just a bird," said Simón.

"You mean a Big Bird?" questioned a frightened Martín.

"No, just a bird," declared Simón, "just a plain and ordinary bird. Okay?"

"I'm scared," said Martín.

"Stop being such a baby," declared Simón. "I already told you, there is no such thing as El Big Bird!"

Just then two huge clawed feet, armed with razor-sharp talons the size of kitchen knives, grabbed a firm hold of little Simón's shoulders and scooped him off the ground!

"Help," Simón cried out, "help me, Martín!"

Martín was too frightened to move. All he could do was watch and scream in terror as a giant bird with leather wings flew away with his older brother Simón clutched tightly between its sharp claws! Martín knew that Simón had become a late-night snack for El Big Bird. All that little Martín could do now was hope that it did not come back for dessert!

Los Chupacabras

"Sorry, boy," said Leo as he fed his pet German shepherd Loco a can of dog food for dinner. "Mom is still pretty upset about you digging up those big holes in her garden. She said we had to keep you chained up until she feels that you have learned your lesson and changed your ways."

Loco gave out a loud sigh as if he had understood what his master Leo had just said.

"Yeah, I know it's hard, boy," said Leo. "I told Mom that digging holes is what dogs do, but she just doesn't understand. I think she's a cat person at heart."

Loco raised his front paws and placed them over the top of his head, in what appeared to be a gesture of frustration.

"Leo, do you see that?" asked Lupe, Leo's younger brother. Leo turned and noticed what looked like red, blue, and yellow blinking lights soaring across the night sky.

"It's flying too low to be a plane," said Leo.

"Yeah," replied Lupe. "It's kind of weird. What do you think it is?" he asked.

"I don't know, but it seems to be heading our way," commented Leo, noticing that the blinking lights seemed to

be moving in their direction.

"Hey, Leo, have you noticed how much the goats are starting to act up?" asked Lupe, noticing for the first time how restless the herd had become. "Even old Loco has begun to growl and bark at the sky."

Leo did not answer Lupe. He was too busy staring at the blinking red, blue, and yellow lights that were now circling above where they both stood. That is when Leo noticed the flying metallic ship shaped like an egg.

Leo came to a sudden conclusion. "It's a UFO!" he cried out.

"I don't believe it," declared Lupe frightened. "It's a real UFO!"

"The goats," cried out Leo, "it's hovering over the goats!"

Suddenly a yellow beam of light shot out from the center of the UFO and hit the ground a few feet away from where the goats had been grazing moments earlier. In the yellow beam of light the boys could see a dozen green-skinned and red-eyed monsters the size of children descend down in the fetal position. They all sprung to life the minute their three-toed feet touched the ground.

"*¡Los chupacabras!*" screamed Leo. "And they look like they are getting ready to attack!"

Leo and Lupe could not believe what their eyes were seeing. They too had heard the many tales of the green-skinned space aliens that fed on goat's blood, but had considered them to be stories and nothing more.

The space aliens descended on the goats like a swarm of locusts, sinking their razor-sharp teeth into the animals' neck arteries!

"They are going to kill all the goats!" cried out Lupe. "If we don't stop them, there won't be any left!"

But it was too late, for within seconds *los chupacabras* had decimated the entire herd, leaving nothing more than their blood-drained carcasses lying on the ground. That's when the green-skinned and red-eyed monsters turned their attention to the two young boys. *Los chupacabras* were still hungry and perfectly willing to settle for the blood of two small humans as well!

"Run!" Leo cried out. He and Lupe ran as fast as their feet could carry them, but *los chupacabras* ran just a little bit faster! They descended on the two boys, knocking them down to the ground. It seemed nothing in the world could save them now. The beasts seemed poised to drink their young victims' blood!

"Woof, woof!" The loud barking sounds of Loco the dog suddenly rang out, and the two boys turned to see the form of their pet German shepherd growling menacingly at *los chupacabras*. A metal chain was dangling from his neck. Loco had broken the chain that had restrained him and come to his young masters' aid!

"Woof, woof!" barked Loco, advancing on *los chupacabras*, who seemed hesitant to tangle with the dog.

"Grrr," snarled Loco, who then leapt at *los chupacabras*, biting one in the arm and then another in the leg.

Loco acted like if he was possessed. *Los chupacabras* could do nothing more than beat a hasty retreat as they were beamed back up to their UFO! In the blink of an eye, *los chupacabras* and their spacecraft were both gone.

"Loco, you saved us!" declared Leo and Lupe as they hugged him.

"You're a hero, Loco," said Leo, "a real-live hero!"

The boy's dog Loco was never tied up again. After that night, he was always allowed to run free, no matter how many times he dug up Mom's garden.

About Xavier Garza

I come from a family of storytellers. My grandfather Ventura told my cousins and me many *cucuy* stories. Each of his tales began with those famous words that storytellers have always said, "This is suppose to have happened a long time ago to a friend of a friend who swears that the story is true."

My grandmother Braulia, not one to be outdone, would also tell us her own *cucuy* stories as she worked over a hot stove preparing dinner for the family. I remember her telling me the tale of "La Llorona," for what must have been the fiftieth time as she spread refried beans across a steaming hot flour tortilla. The story still held the same grip on me as it did the first time I ever heard it.

"The Devil at the Dance," "La Llorona," "*Los Duendes,*" "*Las Lechuzas,*" were stories that filled my head with incredible images of fantasy, drama, mystery, horror and excitement as a child. Later they would serve as inspiration for my work as both an author and an artist. They taught me the difference between right and wrong, warning me often of the dire consequences that awaited all "bad," little boys and girls that paid no heed to their parents warnings. Now, as an adult, I have realized that these wonderful stories are more than just stories, they are a piece of our culture, they are our own *Grimms Fairy tales,* representing our beliefs, ideals, and ideas.

With this, my own collection of *cucuy* stories I seek to do what other storytellers such as Juan Sauvageau, "Stories that must not die," have been doing for years. My humble contribution is to ensure that these wonderful stories will be around in years to come for future generations to enjoy.